A STORY OF PLYMOUTH'S PASTies

Emma Lawrence and Oliver Stephens
Illustrated by Roz Best

Pasties in the Past

Can you remember the very first time you had a pasty? People in the South West have been eating them since the dawn of time... well, perhaps not quite that long, but nobody really knows when the first one was made.

Most of us associate pasties with Cornwall, and with good reason. Cornish tin, copper and arsenic miners ate homemade pasties for crib or crowst (that's lunch to you and me) from the early 1800s onwards. It wasn't just wholesome and filling, but a good way to use up leftovers from the night before too.

Superstitious miners had to be careful of pesky little spirits called Knockers or Buccas who were supposed to live in the mines. The spirits knocked on the walls to warn the miners of any danger, but if the miners forgot to feed them their leftover pasty crusts, the sneaky creatures could make the mineshaft collapse, trapping the miners hundreds of metres underground!

Today we know that arsenic is a poisonous chemical. In the 19th century, however, it was mixed into medicines, used for making glass, colouring wallpaper, and...

LADIES!

YOU CAN BE BEAUTIFUL!

Even the coarsest, most repulsively disfigured skin can become unrivalled in beauty through the regular use of

DR COOPER'S *Arsenic Perfume*

ARSENIC

The mines were dank, dark and dingy places with no electricity, no natural light, and no running water to wash the arsenic and sulphur from the miners' filthy hands. So the crimp (the curled edge of the pasty) was used as a handle to make sure the men didn't poison themselves. Who'd have thought that an extra fold of pastry could save a miner's life?

It wasn't only the miners who ate pasties though: farmers, blacksmiths, brewers and just about any other worker you could think of would take a pasty for lunch. Children often carried pasties to school with them too; if the school didn't have a stove to heat them on they could ask a friendly shopkeeper to keep their pasties warm till lunchtime.

After all, a pasty was, and still is, the perfect portable meal:

You don't need to worry about cutlery or a plate.

Pasties stay warm for ages, but we can quickly reheat them if they do go cold.

And they taste great!

They're easy to carry.

However, there was one group of men who would NEVER take a pasty to work with them. Fishermen believed it was bad luck to have pasties on their boats. If they found one aboard they'd cut the ends off "to let the wind blow the devil out"!

When the mines closed down and the Cornish miners sailed off to find work around the world, they took their recipes with them. Maybe that's why, today, everyone associates pasties with Cornwall. But over the border in Devon, they were just as important.

Cast it to the waters!

The Posh Pasty

In 2006, local historian, Dr Todd Gray, was leafing through an old account book in the Plymouth and West Devon Records Office, when he discovered a list of expenses that could only relate to pasties. News soon spread to Cornwall, London and then around the world. Why was everyone so interested? Well, because this was the earliest written record of pasty ingredients; it had been found in Plymouth and it was 236 years older than Cornwall's first record of a pasty! Cornish people weren't happy, and the newspapers loved it! They talked of 'Pasty Wars' and enjoyed stirring up the old rivalry between the two counties.

Venison's deer isn't it?

The historic pasties included expensive venison (deer meat) and must have been made for a posh party; the list also includes 'claret' and 'red wine' – drinks ordinary working people could never have afforded.

The list dated back to 1510, a time when Henry VIII was on the English throne and pinching a pasty might have earned you a whipping. Henry probably liked pasties too. We know his favourite wife, Jane Seymour, ate them. In July 1537, perhaps hoping to get into the queen's good books, John Hussee sent Jane "three pasties of the red deer, caused to be baked without lard".

Pasties in Print

Pasties are so popular, whole books have been written about them (not just this one). They've been mentioned by some very famous literary legends:

I mention pasties in my story called 'The Cook's Tale'.

I wrote about pasties in three of my plays.

I talk about pasties nearly fifty times in my famous diary.

Samuel Pepys witnessed the Great Fire of London in 1666 and wrote about it.

Geoffrey Chaucer English poet from the 14th century – he wrote *The Canterbury Tales*.

William Shakespeare – often called the greatest writer of all time.

The People's Pasty

The word pasty originally referred to a pie you could eat without a plate, and it wasn't just for posh people. Ordinary working people probably ate pasties in the 1500s, though it's unlikely they used the same recipe as the rich, and they wouldn't have written about it because:

- they probably couldn't write
- they didn't have much spare time
- they may have referred to pasties by another name!

If you've ever been to a football or rugby match in Devon or Cornwall, you've probably heard the cry:

Oi, oi, oi!

OGGY OGGY OGGY!

Once upon a time, this cry was used to call miners up for their pasty lunch. The same cry even echoed around the Devonport Dockyard until just over sixty years ago.

Mr Tripp, from Camel's Head, had a daytime job, but at night he became… the Oggy Man! Catching the bus at around 8pm, he would head down to the Albert Gate entrance to the Dockyard with a wooden barrel filled with hot pasties, to sell to the Dockyard workers as they finished their shifts.

His cry of "Oggy, oggy, oggy!" was the sound of home for many a homesick sailor, in fact, he was so well known that in 1959, a folk singer, called Cyril Tawney, even wrote a song about him. But by then the Oggy Man was long gone. Wartime bombs had cleared a space opposite his pitch where mobile snack bars parked up, putting Mr Tripp out of business.

It was the end of what might have been a very long tradition; some say an Oggy Man has stood at the Dockyard gates since they first opened back in 1690!

Oggy (or oggie) is navy slang for a pasty and it probably comes from the Cornish word 'hoggan' or 'hogan' meaning, you guessed it… pasty!

Ask for an oggy in Plymouth today and it's likely you'll still get a pasty. But around Devonport there are some other names you could try:

- a rat in a coffin
- an elephant's toenail
- a janner kebab
- a Devonport mouth organ.

When I said I wanted a rat in a coffin… I didn't mean I wanted a rat in a coffin!

An Oggy in Guz

Devonport grew up around the Dockyard, and by the early 1900s, it was the largest town in Devon. If you'd strolled the streets 100 years ago, you'd have passed cinemas, department stores, pubs, hotels and theatres. There was a bustling market selling just about everything, from fresh fish and fragrant flowers to meat from the local abattoir. Even the street corners were dotted with shellfish, hot chestnut and, of course, pasty stalls.

For a sailor returning to Guz* after months of being at sea, any fresh food was a welcome change. The daily menu on board ship was mainly pickled meat, preserved vegetables and ship's biscuit, so sailors looked forward to their first 'oggy'; it was a sign that they were truly home at last.

Of course, it wasn't just the sailors who needed feeding. Ship builders, engineers and other Dockyard workers enjoyed a pasty when they clocked off their shifts. In fact, pasty sales flourished all around Devonport.

When the First World War ended, many families were left without a father to bring in a wage. To make matters worse, the Depression struck around the world in the 1930s and thousands of people lost their jobs. When the Dockyard hooters signalled the end of the day, workers were often greeted at the gates by hungry children asking, "Any lefts, Sir?" Some mothers had to resort to feeding their children at soup kitchens, where they could buy a pint of soup for tuppence (less than one pence in today's money).

James William Selleck trained as a baker and set up a business in Plymouth in the 1900s. After his wife asked him to make her a pasty, Mr Selleck suddenly realised he could be selling them too. During the First World War, Selleck supplied pasties to the troops stationed locally. Later, in the 1940s, he opened a restaurant in an old burned-out chapel in Ebrington Street where his pastry press was the talk of the town: it could push out seven equal portions of pastry at one time, to make a faster pasty!

*Guz is the Navy's nickname for Plymouth – perhaps because the local sailors liked 'guzzling' pasties!

Plymouth's Pasty-makers

For a filling, good-value meal, you could also buy pasties for tuppence each. On the other hand, anyone with a good family recipe and enough room to bake them at home could make some easy money selling pasties. And in the years before and during the Second World War, you could buy them just about anywhere in Plymouth. Uglow's boasted that their business had started baking bread (and maybe pasties too) in 1830, while S. Stephens and Risdon Ltd had two cafes in Devonport and 12 bakeries around the city.

Baking and confectionary shops were often family-run businesses that cared about their customers. Some of the best-loved pasty-makers even made local history, by becoming a town councillor, mayor, or even lord mayor of Plymouth. Richard Risdon must have liked his pasties, as he weighed in as Plymouth's heaviest mayor in 1900!

Richard Risdon **Richard Uglow** **Solomon Stephens**

Bicycle Boys

If you couldn't get to a pasty shop, the pasties might come to you! In the 1930s boys leaving school at 14 could get a job delivering pasties to Plymouth's leisure hotspots, including pubs, football matches, cinemas and even the queue for the visiting circus!

A Brand New Bakery Business

Down the road from Devonport, in the 1920s, one particular family kitchen was a hive of baking activity.

The kitchen was in Stoke and it belonged to the Dewdney family. At the age of 21, the oldest son, Ivor, was baking batch upon batch of pasties. Fresh from the oven, he'd load them into a barrow and sell them around the local pubs.

Ivor had big ideas for his pasties and, attracted by the bright city lights, he took off for London to try his hand at working in wholesale whilst baking his own pasties to sell on the side.

William Dewdney and Jessie Cann married and had five children. Their three sons, Ivor, Ron and William (who went by his middle name of Clifford) would all end up in the pasty business.

Sadly, outside of the South West, pasties didn't seem so popular, and Ivor's business venture was not a success. If he was disappointed it didn't show, nor did he let a lack of money hold him back; he just sold his dad's car (no one knows what William Dewdney had to say about that!) to buy ingredients and set up a mini pasty-making factory in some disused stables in Plympton. Before long, he was marching his barrow, full of fresh pasties, in and out of the pubs in Plympton.

In the 1920s the historic town of Plympton boasted its own cinema, a regular motorbus and a railway station.

By 1932, Ivor had his own general store at 1 Albert Road, Devonport. A few years later, in 1935, he was able to open his first proper pasty shop in the centre of Plymouth. The shop in King Street was the first in Plymouth to sell nothing but pasties and pies.

Ivor's father, William Dewdney, had a full-time job as a chauffeur for Major Clifford Tozer, but he may have dabbled in pasties too. Ivor's brother Clifford trained as a pastry chef and was a dab-hand at pasty-making. With his dad's help, by 1939, he had opened a shop at 14 High Street, Devonport – very handy for the Dockyard.

But 1939 was also the year that the Second World War broke out…

People told Ivor that a business selling just pasties and pies would never work. He was determined to prove them wrong!

Keep Calm and Carry On

James Clifford Tozer became 'Major Tozer' during the First World War and afterwards served as a local councillor, Mayor of Plymouth, and Chairman of Plymouth Argyle Football Club! He became 'Sir Clifford' in 1939. The Tozer's family-run store in Devonport was flattened during the Blitz, but in business again just one week later!

Among other duties, the Home Guard were expected to patrol local factories and railway stations, clear up after an air raid, help rescue victims from bombed-out buildings and learn weapons skills.

Preparations for war had already begun. Local shops were selling blackout curtains and metal boxes to keep valuables safe during bombing raids. Ugly air-raid shelters were ruining people's gardens and children were being evacuated from the larger cities to the safety of smaller towns and cities… like Plymouth! At first, no one realised Plymouth was in danger.

Everyone was expected to do their part and, in true wartime spirit, both Ivor and Clifford took on extra responsibilities. Ivor signed up for the Home Guard. After a full day's work, he would set off on his night-time patrol. With no time to go home between shifts, each day his wife, Ivy, brought in fresh clothes for his transformation from pasty maker to city patroller.

Clifford trained in Yelverton as a firefighter but kept his shop open too. Tackling a fire in Devonport one night, he had to watch helplessly as heat from the flames melted the margarine in his bakery and it trickled down the road!

Business in the Blitz

Always busy during wartime, the Dockyard made Plymouth and Devonport prime targets for the enemy, and the first bombs fell on Plymouth in July 1940. They destroyed eight houses on Swilly Road, leaving locals scared for their lives. Much worse was yet to come however; on the night of 20th March 1941 the Plymouth Blitz began. Plymouth soon earned the title of 'worst blitzed city in Britain'. In 59 horrific bomb attacks, 1,172 people lost their lives and thousands more were seriously injured.

The blackout meant that buildings had to be kept dark at night. There was no street lighting and car headlights had to be dimmed so that they were practically useless. The blackout was supposed to stop enemy planes finding a target to bomb, but it actually caused many accidental deaths and injuries.

Ivor had a lucky escape one night, driving down Embankment Road to pick up supplies. On his way back the road was closed because of an unexploded bomb. Earlier that night, he'd driven along that very road and hadn't seen the bomb – luckily he hadn't crashed into it either!

Ivor's King Street shop stayed open throughout the war, sometimes until 11 o'clock at night – people still came to buy pasties in the dark! And with so many troops stationed around Plymouth, there was never a shortage of customers.

Amazingly, King Street was one of the few streets in Plymouth's city centre to avoid the bombing. Other shops weren't so lucky but despite the devastation, businesses were quickly up and running again.

Rationing and Rubble

Food rationing began in 1940 and some pasty ingredients became hard to find. Although Ivor got his meat and potatoes directly from local farmers and butchers, he often had to travel up to Bristol Docks just to buy onions – a round trip of 250 miles! With no dual carriageways in those days, the journey usually took the whole day.

Corned Beef Pasties Anyone?

Devonport resident, Mary Lacy, remembers her mum getting up at five in the morning to bake a big batch of pasties to sell from their shop! With extra workers at the Dockyard, pasties were more popular than ever. Mary's mum got most of her vegetables from Cornwall but sometimes couldn't get hold of the meat. American troops stationed nearby offered tins of corned beef, so she popped that in her pasties instead!

Sometimes Ivor had to take his family along for the ride.

KEEP DANCING AND WE'LL WIN THE WAR

SERVICEMEN'S DANCE
FRIDAY 8TH MAY 1942
Market Hall, Market Road, Plympton

To keep morale high during the war, Ivor and his friends often organised dances for servicemen.

By the time the war ended in 1945, large parts of Plymouth were little more than piles of rubble and debris. Instead of rebuilding the city as it had been before, the council drew up fantastic new plans for the city centre. Some of the streets that survived the Blitz now had to be knocked down; King Street was one of them.

WEDDING OF THE WEEK

09 AUG 1941
MARRIED last Saturday, this happy couple enjoyed a wedding breakfast of an Ivor Dewdney pasty followed by a quick trip to the cinema, before the groom headed back to war in the evening.

Post-war Pasties

On 26th June 1957, Ivor's old shop closed for the last time, but the very next morning a brand new one opened at 99 Cornwall Street. His fifteen employees were more than happy to move with him. The new, specially designed premises included a staff canteen, staff kitchen (with its own cook!) and even a roof garden. The ovens, mixers and moulding machines were bang up-to-date too.

The new shop at 99 Cornwall Street

Parts of Devonport had been completely flattened during the Blitz and new plans to rebuild its once busy streets were sadly put on hold. After the war, Clifford moved his business to Millbridge, Stoke – but he didn't forget the Dockyard. Every day, man-with-a-van Mr Richardson parked up at St Levan's Gate to sell Clifford Dewdney pasties to the Dockyard workers. The pasties proved so popular that Clifford started making plans to build his new shop right opposite the gate.

A BIG Tradition

Back in the 1950s when the circus was in town, Clifford baked a massive pasty to celebrate. It was six feet long! Today, a Ron Dewdney 'Whopper' isn't as big but it's still the size of sixteen medium pasties. One or two Whoppers have even been taken to 10 Downing Street in support of the Dockyard workers.

Penny Pasties

To celebrate their 60th anniversary, in 1995, Ivor Dewdney's offered loyal fans six pasties for six pence. Hungry customers queued for over two hours and bought a total of 12,127 pasties!

Crimping queen, Muriel Champion, started working at Ivor Dewdney's when she was just 14. She hung up her apron for the last time in 1993, having made 10 million pasties… enough for everyone in Plymouth to have 40 pasties each!

It's thought that Clifford and Ivor worked on the plans for their shops together, but tragedy struck for Clifford when his wife, Freda, died in 1954. Just three years later Clifford died too. They left three young daughters.

Up until then, Ron Dewdney had kept out of the family businesses and got himself a job with the gas board. But with Clifford gone and his new shop underway, Ron stepped in to keep the business going. The pasties sold so well that Ron had to extend the shop in the 1970s. Ron is also long gone now but the pasty recipe remains the same, and the shop is still standing.

Feeding the Troops

Sailors today look forward to their ten o'clock break. It's called 'stand easy' or 'Jack's breakfast', and for those lucky enough to be docked at Devonport that means a pint of milk and a hot pasty! Ron Dewdney's reckon they've supplied pasties, day and night, to just about every ship that's docked in Devonport since 1960!

When the 'pass boat' takes supplies out to the ships that dock in the Sound, there's often a fresh batch of pasties on board to feed the hungry sailors. Today's owner is so familiar to captain and crew of the HMS *Boxer*, that once it almost set sail while he was still on board!

Ivor Dewdney's has a strong connection with the forces too, having sent huge parcels of pasties to British troops around the world. In 2006, the company flew 800 pasties – weighing around half a ton – to Afghanistan to help boost the morale of the Royal Marines stationed there.

Keeping it in the Family:

Both Dewdney companies have kept the family involved from a very early age:

*   Clifford's daughters still remember standing on boxes to help egg-wash the pasties.

*   when Ivor's Cornwall Street Shop opened, it was his eleven-year-old son, Paul, who gave the opening speech.

Ivor died in 1970, but his grandchildren are still in charge of business today. Ron's shop was sold to one of his loyal employees in 1990 and his family still run the business.

Ron's and Ivor's are, and have always been, two separate businesses; they even prepare their pasties differently. Ron's uses thin shortcrust pastry, while Ivor's have always used what's called a 'Scotch' puff pastry.

But whatever their methods, both companies have produced award-winning pasties and still share the same values today as their founders did back in the 1930s.

What to Put in a Pasty

There are many more pasty shops in Plymouth today and many new fillings around. Fancy a chicken tikka, banana or chocolate pasty? One bakery in Cornwall even fills their pasties with grey squirrel meat!

Traditionally, family cooks would put just about anything they could find in the larder into a pasty, especially leftovers from dinner the day before. Meat was important and chicken, pork, rabbit and mutton have all been used, but when no meat was to hand vegetables would do.

We made pasties with spinach and parsley.

I liked them best with pilchards and cream.

Ugh—fish in a pasty? No thanks!

We like 'tiddy oggies' – filled with potatoes and maybe a bit of cream. Mmm.

There's a story that poor families used to spit out the bacon from Monday's pasty and use it again on Tuesday. This way, one pasty had the bacon flavour and the other had the meat!

Sweet AND Savoury?

People disagree over whether pasties were ever made with a savoury end, filled with meat and vegetables, and a sweet end, filled with fruit or jam. We know that two-course pasties did exist, though, because some people in the South West still make them today!

Leftover pastry was often used for a jam roly-poly pudding or a sweet 'windy' pasty, which was simple to make. Here's how to do it:

Butter leftover scraps of pastry, fold over and cook in the oven till they puff up. Open them out and spread with cream, jam or stewed fruit. Yum!

A windy pasty

One way to eat a Plymouth pasty: split it open and pop a sausage on top, then smother it in tomato sauce. It's called a Ron Dewdney Special – and nicknamed a 'Bosun's* Mate' by the sailors who made it popular.

Many Plymouth families have their own version of the pasty recipe, passed down through the generations; some spread the pastry with butter, others might add a dollop of clotted cream… The Dewdney's even have a special seasoning but they won't tell you what it is – that's a family secret!

Around Plymouth, pasty making was part of family life and one day each week would be 'pasty-making day'. A Barbican resident of the 1950s remembers taking the day off school sometimes to help his grandmother make 13 pasties for the family!

The Classic Pasty

With so many possible pasty ingredients, it seems odd that the Cornish pasty needed protecting – by law! Since 2011, you can only call a pasty 'Cornish' if it has:

a 'D' shape
a side crimp
AT LEAST 12.5% beef
potato, onion, swede and a light seasoning
(salt and plenty of pepper)

And of course, it has to be made in Cornwall! The classic ingredients of the Cornish pasty are available all year around (which is probably why they were used so often) and they provide a filling, nutritious main meal. But the Dewdney family has also been making and selling this type of pasty in Plymouth for over 80 years!

Despite all the arguments about pasties, there's one thing everyone agrees on: a pasty needs strong pastry.

It's thought that the earliest pasties were made with a barley crust. It was rough and tough, and used to hold the ingredients together – you weren't supposed to eat it!

A miner would joke that his pasty had to be so solid that it wouldn't split open if he dropped it down the mineshaft!

*A bosun – short for boatswain – is a ship's officer.

Make a Proper Pasty

Why not have a go at baking your own pasty?

The Classic Pasty

Wash your hands before you start and ask an adult to help.
Makes 6 medium pasties

Pastry
450g plain white bread flour
A pinch of salt
100g margarine or butter
110g lard
Up to 175ml cold water

The Famous Filling
300g beef skirt, or chuck steak,
(you can ask a butcher to prepare it for you)
450g potato
150g swede
150g onion
Salt and black pepper
1 egg, beaten, and kept in a separate bowl
ready to coat, or glaze, the pastry.

To make

Pastry
1. In a bowl, rub the flour, salt, butter and lard together
   with your fingers until they look like fine breadcrumbs.
2. Add the water a little at a time, mixing it in with a blunt
   knife. Then use your fingers to push the mixture into a
   ball – you may not need all the water.
3. Wrap the pastry in cling film and let it chill in the fridge
   while you get on with....

The Famous Filling
1. Preheat the oven to 180°C (gas mark 4) and wipe a
   baking tray with butter or lard.
2. Ask for help to slice the meat and vegetables into thin
   slivers that will cook through quickly. Keep the ingredients
   in separate dishes.
3. Dust a surface with flour and roll the pastry into a long
   sausage shape. Cut it into six pieces.
4. Roll out each piece of pastry separately, until you can
   cover it with a small dinner plate (about 22cm wide).
   Cut round the edge of the plate with a blunt knife, to
   get a neat circle of pastry.
5. Taking one disk at a time, add a layer of swede and onion.
   Sprinkle with plenty of salt and pepper (seasoning). Now
   add a layer of meat and 'season' again. Add the potato on
   top and 'season' again.
6. Brush the edge of the pastry with water. Keeping the filling
   away from the edge, fold half of the pastry over it. Make
   slits in the top to let steam escape when the pasty is hot.